Guest book to celebrate

Happy thoughts

_____

_____

_____

Name _____

Email / Phone _____

Happy thoughts

_____

_____

_____

Name _____

Email / Phone _____

Happy thoughts

_____

_____

_____

Name _____

Email / Phone _____

Happy thoughts

_____

_____

_____

Name _____

Email / Phone _____

～ Happy thoughts ～

....

....

....

Name ....

Email / Phone ....

～ Happy thoughts ～

....

....

....

Name ....

Email / Phone ....

❧❧ Happy thoughts ❧❧

Name

Email / Phone

❧❧ Happy thoughts ❧❧

Name

Email / Phone

❧❧ Happy thoughts ❧❧

....

....

....

Name ....
Email / Phone ....

❧❧ Happy thoughts ❧❧

....

....

....

Name ....
Email / Phone ....

Happy thoughts

Name

Email / Phone

Happy thoughts

Name

Email / Phone

❦ Happy thoughts ❦

....

....

....

Name ....

Email / Phone ....

❦ Happy thoughts ❦

....

....

....

Name ....

Email / Phone ....

Happy thoughts

Name

Email / Phone

Happy thoughts

Name

Email / Phone

Happy thoughts

Name

Email / Phone

Happy thoughts

Name

Email / Phone

Happy thoughts

....

....

....

Name ....

Email / Phone ....

Happy thoughts

....

....

....

Name ....

Email / Phone ....

Happy thoughts

_____

_____

_____

Name _____

Email / Phone _____

Happy thoughts

_____

_____

_____

Name _____

Email / Phone _____

Happy thoughts

_____

_____

_____

Name _____

Email / Phone _____

Happy thoughts

_____

_____

_____

Name _____

Email / Phone _____

Happy thoughts

Name

Email / Phone

Happy thoughts

Name

Email / Phone

Happy thoughts

_____

_____

_____

Name _____

Email / Phone _____

Happy thoughts

_____

_____

_____

Name _____

Email / Phone _____

Happy thoughts

Name

Email / Phone

Happy thoughts

Name

Email / Phone

Happy thoughts

_____

_____

_____

Name _____

Email / Phone _____

Happy thoughts

_____

_____

_____

Name _____

Email / Phone _____

❧ Happy thoughts ❧

....

....

....

Name ....

Email / Phone ....

❧ Happy thoughts ❧

....

....

....

Name ....

Email / Phone ....

Happy thoughts

Name

Email / Phone

Happy thoughts

Name

Email / Phone

Happy thoughts

Name

Email / Phone

Happy thoughts

Name

Email / Phone

Happy thoughts

....

....

....

Name ....

Email / Phone ....

Happy thoughts

....

....

....

Name ....

Email / Phone ....

Happy thoughts

....

....

....

Name ....

Email / Phone ....

Happy thoughts

....

....

....

Name ....

Email / Phone ....

Happy thoughts

Name

Email / Phone

Happy thoughts

Name

Email / Phone

Happy thoughts

Name

Email / Phone

Happy thoughts

Name

Email / Phone

Happy thoughts

Name

Email / Phone

Happy thoughts

Name

Email / Phone

Happy thoughts

_____

_____

_____

Name _____

Email / Phone _____

Happy thoughts

_____

_____

_____

Name _____

Email / Phone _____

Happy thoughts

....

....

....

Name ....

Email / Phone ....

Happy thoughts

....

....

....

Name ....

Email / Phone ....

Happy thoughts

Name

Email / Phone

Happy thoughts

Name

Email / Phone

Happy thoughts

_____

_____

_____

Name _____

Email / Phone _____

Happy thoughts

_____

_____

_____

Name _____

Email / Phone _____

Happy thoughts

Name

Email / Phone

Happy thoughts

Name

Email / Phone

Happy thoughts

_____

_____

_____

Name _____

Email / Phone _____

Happy thoughts

_____

_____

_____

Name _____

Email / Phone _____

❧ Happy thoughts ❧

....

....

....

Name ....

Email / Phone ....

❧ Happy thoughts ❧

....

....

....

Name ....

Email / Phone ....

Happy thoughts

....

....

....

Name ....

Email / Phone ....

Happy thoughts

....

....

....

Name ....

Email / Phone ....

❦ Happy thoughts ❦

....

....

....

Name ....

Email / Phone ....

❦ Happy thoughts ❦

....

....

....

Name ....

Email / Phone ....

Happy thoughts

Name

Email / Phone

Happy thoughts

Name

Email / Phone

Happy thoughts

....

....

....

Name ....

Email / Phone ....

Happy thoughts

....

....

....

Name ....

Email / Phone ....

Happy thoughts

....

....

....

Name ....

Email / Phone ....

Happy thoughts

....

....

....

Name ....

Email / Phone ....

Happy thoughts

Name

Email / Phone

Happy thoughts

Name

Email / Phone

Happy thoughts

Name

Email / Phone

Happy thoughts

Name

Email / Phone

Happy thoughts

Name

Email / Phone

Happy thoughts

Name

Email / Phone

Happy thoughts

....
....
....

Name
Email / Phone

Happy thoughts

....
....
....

Name
Email / Phone

Happy thoughts

Name

Email / Phone

Happy thoughts

Name

Email / Phone

❧❧ Happy thoughts ❧❧

....

....

....

Name ....

Email / Phone ....

❧❧ Happy thoughts ❧❧

....

....

....

Name ....

Email / Phone ....

Happy thoughts

Name

Email / Phone

Happy thoughts

Name

Email / Phone

Happy thoughts

....

....

....

Name ....

Email / Phone ....

Happy thoughts

....

....

....

Name ....

Email / Phone ....

Happy thoughts

Name

Email / Phone

Happy thoughts

Name

Email / Phone

Happy thoughts

Name

Email / Phone

Happy thoughts

Name

Email / Phone

Happy thoughts

Name

Email / Phone

Happy thoughts

Name

Email / Phone

Happy thoughts

_____

_____

_____

Name _____

Email / Phone _____

Happy thoughts

_____

_____

_____

Name _____

Email / Phone _____

Happy thoughts

....

....

....

Name ....

Email / Phone ....

Happy thoughts

....

....

....

Name ....

Email / Phone ....

Happy thoughts

....

....

....

Name ....

Email / Phone ....

Happy thoughts

....

....

....

Name ....

Email / Phone ....

Happy thoughts

Name

Email / Phone

Happy thoughts

Name

Email / Phone

Happy thoughts

_____

_____

_____

Name _____

Email / Phone _____

Happy thoughts

_____

_____

_____

Name _____

Email / Phone _____

❦ Happy thoughts ❦

....

....

....

Name ....

Email / Phone ....

❦ Happy thoughts ❦

....

....

....

Name ....

Email / Phone ....

Happy thoughts

....

....

....

Name ....

Email / Phone ....

Happy thoughts

....

....

....

Name ....

Email / Phone ....

Happy thoughts

....

....

....

Name ....

Email / Phone ....

Happy thoughts

....

....

....

Name ....

Email / Phone ....

❧ Happy thoughts ❧

....

....

....

Name ....

Email / Phone ....

❧ Happy thoughts ❧

....

....

....

Name ....

Email / Phone ....

Happy thoughts

_____

_____

_____

Name _____

Email / Phone _____

Happy thoughts

_____

_____

_____

Name _____

Email / Phone _____

❧ Happy thoughts ❧

....

....

....

Name ....

Email / Phone ....

❧ Happy thoughts ❧

....

....

....

Name ....

Email / Phone ....

Happy thoughts

Name

Email / Phone

Happy thoughts

Name

Email / Phone

Happy thoughts

_____

_____

_____

Name _____

Email / Phone _____

Happy thoughts

_____

_____

_____

Name _____

Email / Phone _____

Happy thoughts

Name

Email / Phone

Happy thoughts

Name

Email / Phone

Happy thoughts

Name

Email / Phone

Happy thoughts

Name

Email / Phone

Happy thoughts

Name

Email / Phone

Happy thoughts

Name

Email / Phone

Happy thoughts

....

....

....

Name ....

Email / Phone ....

Happy thoughts

....

....

Name ....

Email / Phone ....

Happy thoughts

Name

Email / Phone

Happy thoughts

Name

Email / Phone

Happy thoughts

....

....

....

Name ....

Email / Phone ....

Happy thoughts

....

....

....

Name ....

Email / Phone ....

Happy thoughts

Name

Email / Phone

Happy thoughts

Name

Email / Phone

Happy thoughts

Name

Email / Phone

Happy thoughts

Name

Email / Phone

Happy thoughts

Name

Email / Phone

Happy thoughts

Name

Email / Phone

Happy thoughts

Name

Email / Phone

Happy thoughts

Name

Email / Phone

Happy thoughts

Name

Email / Phone

Happy thoughts

Name

Email / Phone

Happy thoughts

Name

Email / Phone

Happy thoughts

Name

Email / Phone

Happy thoughts

Name

Email / Phone

Happy thoughts

Name

Email / Phone

Happy thoughts

....

....

....

Name ....

Email / Phone ....

Happy thoughts

....

....

....

Name ....

Email / Phone ....

Happy thoughts

Name

Email / Phone

Happy thoughts

Name

Email / Phone

Happy thoughts

....

....

....

Name ....

Email / Phone ....

Happy thoughts

....

....

....

Name ....

Email / Phone ....

Happy thoughts

Name

Email / Phone

Happy thoughts

Name

Email / Phone

Happy thoughts

Name

Email / Phone

Happy thoughts

Name

Email / Phone

Happy thoughts

Name

Email / Phone

Happy thoughts

Name

Email / Phone

Happy thoughts

....

....

....

Name ....

Email / Phone ....

Happy thoughts

....

....

....

Name ....

Email / Phone ....

Happy thoughts

Name

Email / Phone

Happy thoughts

Name

Email / Phone

Happy thoughts

_____

_____

_____

Name _____

Email / Phone _____

Happy thoughts

_____

_____

_____

Name _____

Email / Phone _____

Happy thoughts

Name

Email / Phone

Happy thoughts

Name

Email / Phone

Happy thoughts

Name

Email / Phone

Happy thoughts

Name

Email / Phone

⚜ Happy thoughts ⚜

....

Name ....

Email / Phone ....

⚜ Happy thoughts ⚜

....

....

....

Name ....

Email / Phone ....

❦ Happy thoughts ❦

....

....

....

Name ....

Email / Phone ....

❦ Happy thoughts ❦

....

....

....

Name ....

Email / Phone ....

Happy thoughts

Name

Email / Phone

Happy thoughts

Name

Email / Phone

Happy thoughts

....

....

Name ....

Email / Phone ....

Happy thoughts

....

....

Name ....

Email / Phone ....

❧ Happy thoughts ❧

Name

Email / Phone

❧ Happy thoughts ❧

Name

Email / Phone

❦ Happy thoughts ❦

....

....

Name ....

Email / Phone ....

❦ Happy thoughts ❦

....

....

Name ....

Email / Phone ....

Happy thoughts

Name

Email / Phone

Happy thoughts

Name

Email / Phone

Happy thoughts

....

....

....

Name ....

Email / Phone ....

Happy thoughts

....

....

....

Name ....

Email / Phone ....

Happy thoughts

Name

Email / Phone

Happy thoughts

Name

Email / Phone

Happy thoughts

....

....

....

Name ....

Email / Phone ....

Happy thoughts

....

....

....

Name ....

Email / Phone ....

❦ Happy thoughts ❦

....

....

....

Name ....

Email / Phone ....

❦ Happy thoughts ❦

....

....

....

Name ....

Email / Phone ....

Happy thoughts

_____

_____

_____

Name _____

Email / Phone _____

Happy thoughts

_____

_____

_____

Name _____

Email / Phone _____

Happy thoughts

Name

Email / Phone

Happy thoughts

Name

Email / Phone

Happy thoughts

_____

_____

_____

Name _____

Email / Phone _____

Happy thoughts

_____

_____

_____

Name _____

Email / Phone _____

Happy thoughts

....

....

....

Name ....

Email / Phone ....

Happy thoughts

....

....

....

Name ....

Email / Phone ....

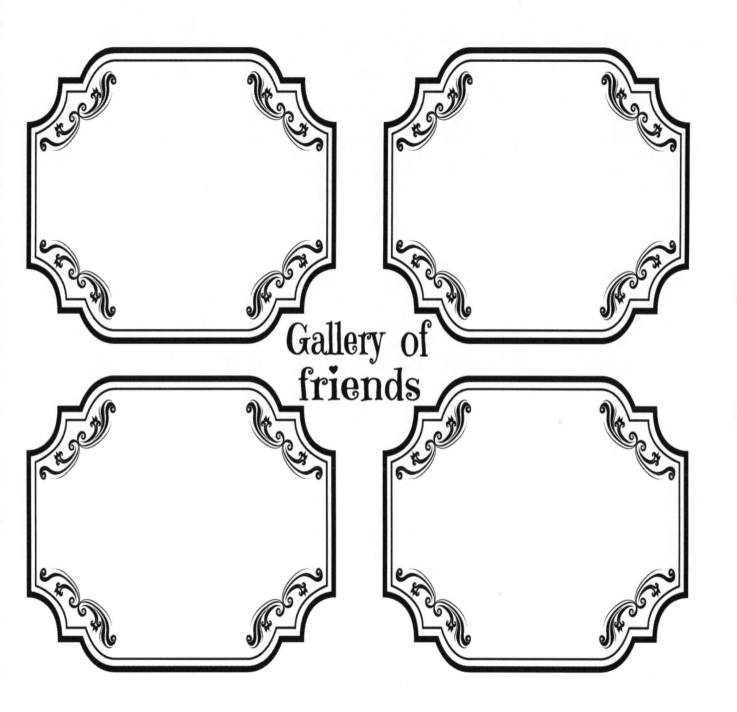

Gallery of
friends

Gallery of
friends

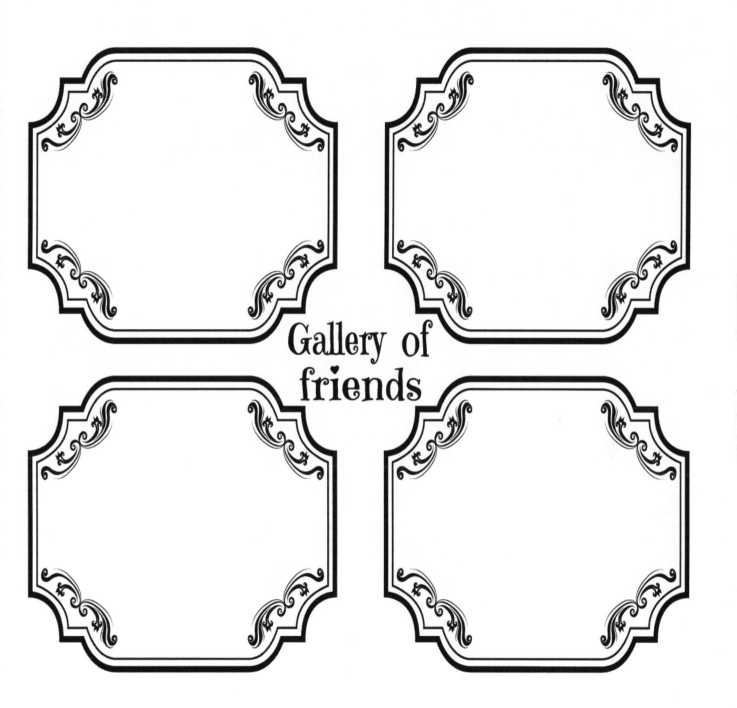

Gallery of
friends

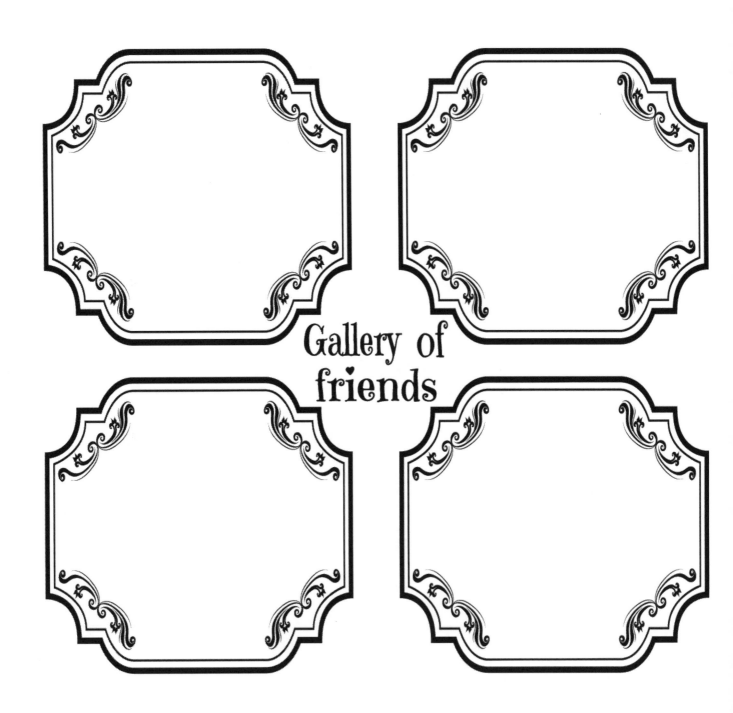

Gallery of
friends

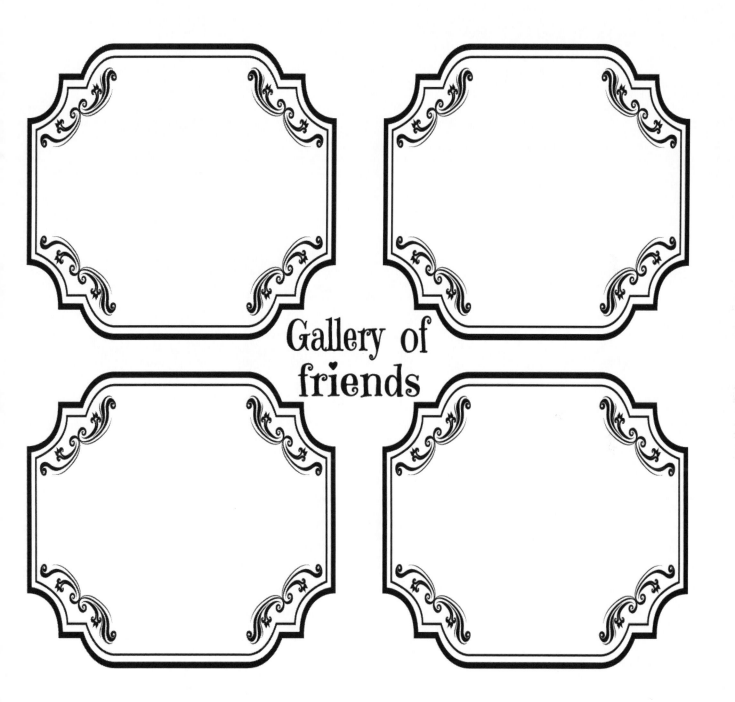

Gallery of
♥ friends

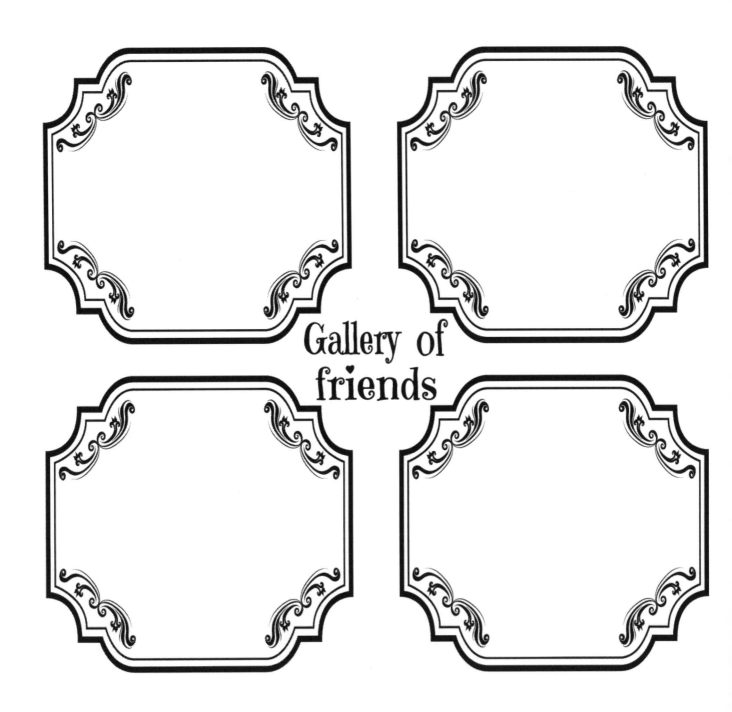

Gallery of
friends

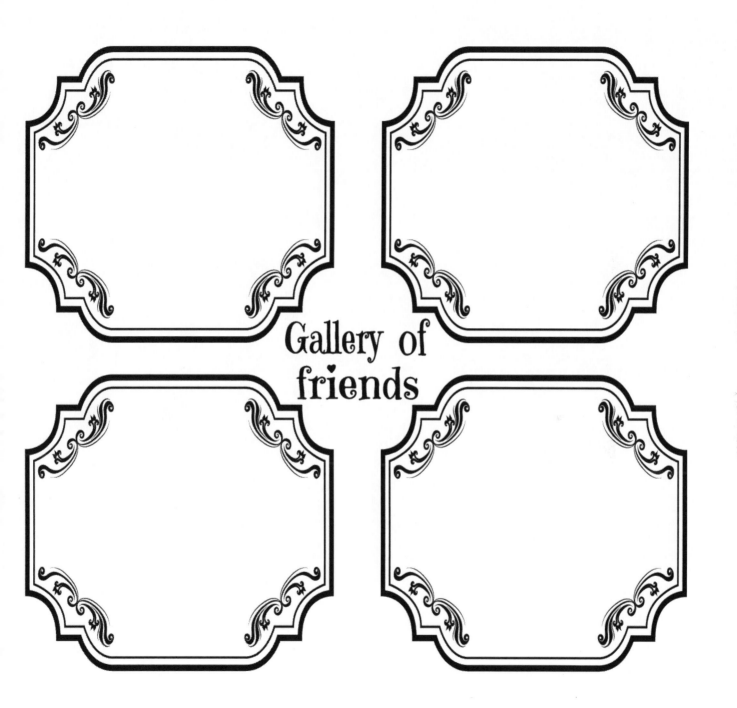

Gallery of
♥ friends

Gallery of
friends

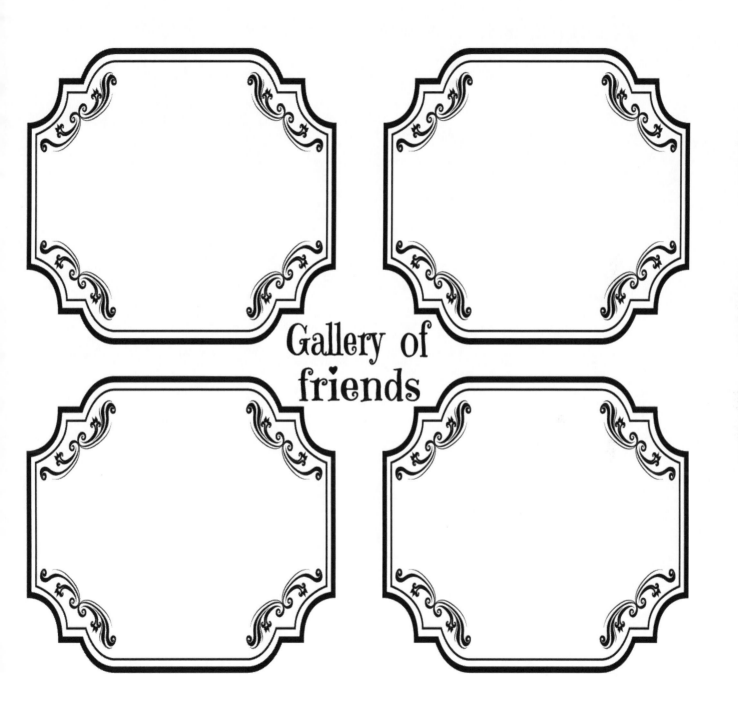

Gallery of
friends

Gallery of
friends

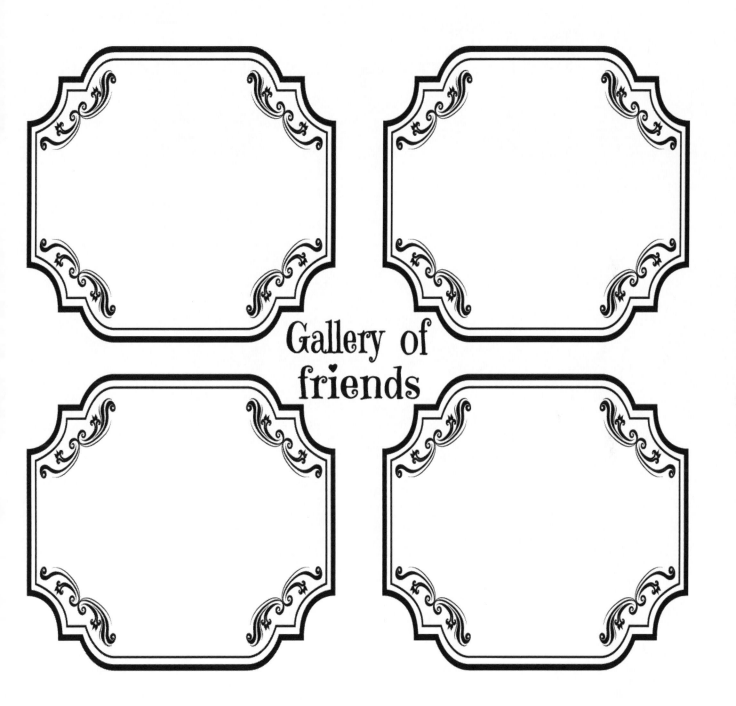

Gallery of
friends

Gift List

Guest name	gift items
....	....
....	....
....	....
....	....
....	....
....	....
....	....
....	....
....	....
....	....
....	....
....	....

Gift List

Guest name

gift items

....

....

....

....

....

....

....

....

....

....

....

....

Gift List

Guest name	gift items
....	....
....	....
....	....
....	....
....	....
....	....
....	....
....	....
....	....
....	....
....	....
....	....

Gift List

Guest name	gift items
....	....
....	....
....	....
....	....
....	....
....	....
....	....
....	....
....	....
....	....
....	....
....	....

Gift List

Guest name	gift items
....	....
....	....
....	....
....	....
....	....
....	....
....	....
....	....
....	....
....	....
....	....
....	....

Gift List

Guest name	gift items
....	....
....	....
....	....
....	....
....	....
....	....
....	....
....	....
....	....
....	....
....	....
....	....

Gift List

Guest name	gift items
....	....
....	....
....	....
....	....
....	....
....	....
....	....
....	....
....	....
....	....
....	....
....	....

Gift List

Guest name	gift items
....	....
....	....
....	....
....	....
....	....
....	....
....	....
....	....
....	....
....	....
....	....
....	....

Gift List

Guest name	gift items
....	....
....	....
....	....
....	....
....	....
....	....
....	....
....	....
....	....
....	....
....	....
....	....

Made in United States
Orlando, FL
09 May 2023

32954461R00067